Belle

By Elizabeth Mills

Illustrated by Jacqueline Rogers

Cartwheel
·B·O·O·K·S·®

SCHOLASTIC INC.

New York   Toronto   London   Auckland   Sydney
Mexico City   New Delhi   Hong Kong   Buenos Aires

To Kathleen,
Thank you for an amazing partnership!
–E. M.

For the Balkens and Blaze, with lots of love,
–J. R.

Library of Congress Cataloging-in-Publication Data is available.

ISBN-13: 978-0-545-06862-8
ISBN-10: 0-545-06862-2

Copyright © 2007 by Reeves International, Inc.

All rights reserved. Published by Scholastic Inc.
BREYER, STABLEMATES, and BREYER logos are trademarks and/or
registered trademarks of Reeves International, Inc.
SCHOLASTIC, CARTWHEEL BOOKS, and associated logos
are trademarks and/or registered trademarks of Scholastic Inc.
Lexile is a registered trademark of MetaMetrics, Inc.

10 9 8 7 6 5 4 3 2 1   09 10 11 12 13

Printed in the U.S.A.
This edition first printing, December 2008

Table of Contents

The Big City

Emmy Johnson lived in a tall apartment building in a big city. She used to live in the country. The country was slow and quiet. The city was busy and loud.

Emmy missed the country.

Emmy also missed riding. In the country, she had a horse of her own. Her horse's name was Dancer. But her parents had to give Dancer away when they moved to the city.

Emmy didn't like the city at all.

One December day, Emmy and her parents were in a big park. There were lots of people in the park. Some rode bikes. Some ran. Some walked.

Just then, Emmy's mom saw a stable. "Look, Emmy," she said.

Chapter 2

Belle

The stable was called Central Stable. Emmy saw many horses in the barn. Some were big; some were small. Some were brown. Some were black. Some were gray, and some were golden.

A woman came up to Emmy and her parents. "Hello, my name is Sally," she said. "What's your name?"

"I'm Emmy," said Emmy.

"Have you ridden before?" asked Sally.

"Yes," said Emmy. "I used to ride my horse in the country. I miss her a lot!"

"I bet you do," said Sally. "Well, I teach riding here in the park. Take a look around and we'll set up some lessons."

Emmy walked into the stable. She smelled the clean hay and listened to the soft nickering of the horses.

Then Emmy saw a small chestnut horse in a corner stall. She had a white blaze on her nose. She whinnied when Emmy came close.

Sally walked up to Emmy.

"This is Belle," said Sally. "She is an American Quarter Horse. Would you like to ride her?"

"Yes, I'd like that," said Emmy.

"Great," said Sally. "I'll see you soon!"

Noise!

The first lesson started after school two days later. Belle nickered happily when she saw Emmy. But Emmy felt sad. She missed Dancer.

There was another girl in the lesson
named Mary. She rode a Palomino Quarter
Horse named Dixie.

Sally took Mary and Emmy out into the
park. They walked. They trotted.

But Emmy was very nervous. She didn't like all the people. The loud noises and honking cars scared her. She pulled on Belle's reins to make her stop. Belle was confused.

Sally rode next to Emmy. "You don't look happy," Sally said.

"I'm not used to the big city," said Emmy.

"Well, you can trust Belle," said Sally. "She's a great horse!"

Emmy tried to calm down. Just then, a
fire engine drove by with its siren on. Emmy
pulled the reins hard. Belle tossed her head
and Emmy let go of the reins in surprise.

Then some people rode by, laughing loudly. But Belle just stood quietly while Emmy scrambled to pick up her reins.

"I think we've done enough riding for one day," said Sally kindly. "Let's go back to the stable."

For the next few lessons, Emmy was
easily frightened. Sally tried to get Emmy
to trust Belle more, but Emmy just didn't
feel at home in the park.

She held the reins too tightly and felt jumpy during the whole lesson.

Lost!

It was getting much colder now and winter was in the air. The Saturday before Christmas, Sally took Mary and Emmy to ride along some new bridle paths. There were lots of trees and almost no cars. It was quiet and still.

"Let's ride here for a bit," Sally said.

For the first time, Emmy started to relax. It was so quiet, she almost felt like she was home in the country. She remembered how nice it was to ride, and she stroked Belle's neck.

Then a car honked its horn. Emmy started to get scared, but Belle just kept walking quietly.

Little by little, Emmy relaxed.

Sally looked back at Belle and Emmy. "You're riding much better now, Emmy!" Sally said. "Let's try a little canter. There's a nice trail ahead. Stay with us and don't fall behind."

Emmy and Belle picked up a canter. Emmy could see tall buildings in the distance. She thought the city looked beautiful.

She was so busy looking at the city that she didn't see where Sally and Mary went. When Emmy and Belle came around a bend, there was a fork in the path, and Sally and Mary were gone!

Emmy didn't know which way to go.
Belle pulled to the left.

"No, Belle," said Emmy. "I think they went
this way."

She turned Belle to the right and clucked
her tongue. They began to walk down the
path.

After a bit, Emmy looked around. "Where are we?" she asked Belle.

There weren't many people around, and it was starting to get dark. Where were Sally and Mary?

Emmy began to cry. They were lost!

Chapter 5

A Christmas Miracle

Then Emmy realized Belle was turning around. "Do you know the way?" she asked Belle. Belle walked slowly back through the woods. She seemed to know where she was going!

At first, Emmy was still scared, but Belle was not scared at all. Emmy began to relax. Soon she heard a car horn. Then she saw the stable.

"You did it!" she told Belle. "You brought us back home!"

Just then, Sally hurried out of the stable with Emmy's parents. "Thank goodness you're back," said Sally. "We were getting worried, but I knew that Belle would take care of you."

"I'm so sorry, Sally," said Emmy. "I was having so much fun that I forgot to watch where you were going. Then I couldn't see you anymore. I picked the wrong path and got lost. But Belle brought us home."

Belle nickered and nodded her head. Emmy gave her a hug. Then Emmy looked up. Snow was falling. The flakes were turning Belle all white. The city looked glittery and magical.

"I think I might like it here after all," Emmy said to her parents.

"That's wonderful!" said Emmy's mom.

"We have a surprise for you," said Emmy's dad. "We're giving Belle to you for Christmas."

Emmy leaned over and hugged Belle again. "You're the best present I could ever have!" she said.

About the Horse

Facts about American Quarter Horses:

1. American Quarter Horses get their name from their ability to run a quarter of a mile faster than any other horse.

2. American Quarter Horses were originally bred by English colonists in the 1600s.

3. American Quarter Horses come in one of 16 colors.

4. American Quarter Horses were the breed of horse that helped settle the United States of America. They were used to pull wagons, round up cattle, and help cowboys out on the ranches.

5. The American Quarter Horse is the world's most popular breed of horse. Today, nearly five million American Quarter Horses have been registered and can be found in more than 80 countries.

6. The American Quarter Horse Association is the breed registry for all American Quarter Horses around the world. It registers 150,000 American Quarter Horses every year.

Every horse has a story.

READ THEM ALL!

www.scholastic.com • www.breyerhorses.com

SCHOLASTIC

STABLEBLC